PORTVILLE FREE LIBRARY
Portville, New York 14770

W9-BWS-990

DISCARDED FROM THE
PORTVILLE FREE LIBRARY

THE BAG
I'M TAKING
TO GRANDMA'S

by **Shirley Neitzel**

pictures by
Nancy Winslow Parker

Greenwillow Books, New York

For Scott and Jeffrey
—S. N.
For Fats, who likes
to pack bags, too
—N. W. P.

Black pen, watercolor paints,
and colored pencils were used
for the full-color art.
The text type is Seagull.

Grateful acknowledgment is made
to Tyco Toys, Inc., and its subsidiary
Matchbox International Limited ("Dinky
Sunbeam Alpine"); and to Buddy L Inc.,
for permission to illustrate their toy cars
in this book.

Text copyright © 1995
by Shirley Neitzel
Illustrations copyright © 1995
by Nancy Winslow Parker
All rights reserved. No part of this book
may be reproduced or utilized in any
form or by any means, electronic or
mechanical, including photocopying,
recording, or by any information
storage and retrieval system, without
permission in writing from the Publisher,
Greenwillow Books, a division of William
Morrow & Company, Inc., 1350 Avenue
of the Americas, New York, NY 10019.
Printed in Hong Kong by Wing King Tong
First Edition   10 9 8 7 6 5 4 3 2 1

Library of Congress
Cataloging-in-Publication Data
Neitzel, Shirley.
    The bag I'm taking to Grandma's /
by Shirley Neitzel;
pictures by Nancy Winslow Parker.
        p.   cm.
Summary: In cumulative verses and
rebuses a young boy and his mother
have different views on how to pack
a bag for a trip to Grandma's.
ISBN 0-688-12960-9 (trade).
ISBN 0-688-12961-7 (lib. bdg.)
[1. Travel—Fiction.
2. Luggage—Fiction.
3. Rebuses. 4. Stories in rhyme.]
I. Parker, Nancy Winslow, ill. II. Title.
PZ8.3.N34Bag   1995   [E]—dc20
94-4115   CIP   AC

Here is the bag I'm taking to Grandma's.

Septen 9/25/95

Here is my mitt for playing ball

that I'll pack in the  I'm taking

to Grandma's.

Here are my cars (I'm taking them all),

along with my for playing ball,

that I'll pack in the  I'm taking

to Grandma's.

Here is my shuttle with the astronaut crew

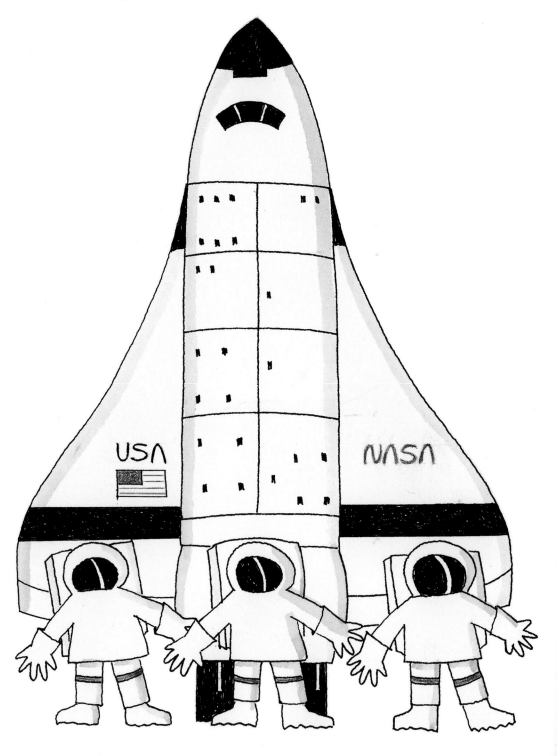

that I'll stash with my (I'm taking them all),

along with my for playing ball,

that I'll pack in the I'm taking

to Grandma's.

Here are the animals, two by two,

that ride in the 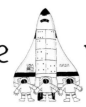 with the astronaut crew

that I'll stash with my (I'm taking them all),

along with my  for playing ball,

that I'll pack in the I'm taking

to Grandma's.

Here is the bunny I sleep with at night,

who guards the  two by two,

that ride in the with the astronaut crew

that I'll stash with my (I'm taking them all),

along with my for playing ball,

that I'll pack in the I'm taking

to Grandma's.

Here is my pillow, fluffy and light,

where I cuddle the  I sleep with at night,

who guards the   two by two,

that ride in the  with the astronaut crew

that I'll stash with my (I'm taking them all),

along with my for playing ball,

that I'll pack in the I'm taking

to Grandma's.

Here is the book I want to read,

propped on my  fluffy and light,

where I cuddle the 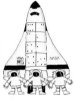 I sleep with at night,

who guards the two by two,

that ride in the  with the astronaut crew

that I'll stash with my  (I'm taking them all),

along with my for playing ball,

that I'll pack in the I'm taking

to Grandma's.

Here is the flashlight I really need

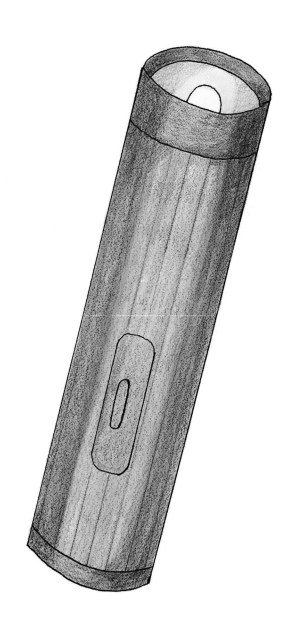

to shine on the I want to read,

propped on my fluffy and light,

where I cuddle the I sleep with at night,

who guards the two by two,

that ride in the with the astronaut crew

that I'll stash with my (I'm taking them all),

along with my  for playing ball,

that I'll pack in the  I'm taking

to Grandma's.

Here is my mother who said, "Ready, hon?

"What's in this bag? It weighs a ton.

"Is this flashlight something you really need?

"Grandma has plenty of books to read.

"You're taking your bunny? Well, all right.

"But leave the pillow for just one night.

"You've got enough animals to stock a zoo!

"Leave them home, and your space shuttle, too.

"Choose one car. You can't take them all.

"And leave your mitt. There's no playing ball in the apartment house at Grandma's.

"Now put in your slippers
and pack these clothes."

"But, Mother,

"I don't have room for those
in the bag I'm taking to Grandma's."

3 2005 0583958 8

E 1-3
Neitzel, Shirley.
  The bag I'm taking to
Grandma's

		DATE DUE		
		DISCARDED FROM THE		
		PORTVILLE FREE LIBRARY		
		6/17/24		

PORTVILLE FREE LIBRARY

PORTVILLE, N. Y.

Member Of
Chautauqua-Cattaraugus Library System